Good Catholic Girl

Novelette

Michael Cooney

ELJ Editions, Ltd. is committed to publishing works of quality and integrity. In that spirit, we are proud to offer this novelette collection to our readers. This novelette is a work of fiction. Names, characters, places, and incidents either are the product of the author's imagination or are used fictitiously, and any resemblance to actual persons, living or dead, business establishments, events, or locales is entirely coincidental.

ISBN: 978-1-941617-56-4

Cover Design by ELJ Editions, Ltd.

ELJ Publications (Imprint)
ELJ Editions, Ltd.
P.O. Box 815
Washingtonville, NY 10992

www.elj-editions.com

Back then Catholic high schools in the Bronx were strictly boys-only, girls-only. The girls wore plaid skirts and went to a nice place like Mount St. Ursula where nuns inspired them to continue their education at nice Catholic colleges like Mount St. Vincent. As to boys, they met them at well-chaperoned mixers where they drank Pepsi out of paper cups, nibbled on Lorna Doones and waited to be asked to dance. And despite what people always said, the nuns did not say "Leave room for the Holy Ghost" when couples were dancing too close. They made sure the lights in the school gym were turned down low and when the girls kissed the boys, the nuns did not react with hysteria. They were romantics, those nuns. They believed in love.

That was girls-only Catholic education. But the boys-only version was fucking sick, as my father put it. That's because those schools were run by Brothers. These guys were not priests, even if they did dress in black suits with funny little white collars. "There's something wrong with all of them" was my father's verdict. "Or else they'd become priests. They're drunks or queer or their father murdered their mother." And this was before it all came out about them raping little boys.

This kind of talk upset my mother, who more or less worshipped anybody called to the service of the Lord. Priests, bishops, nuns, brothers, the Pope for Christ's sake, they were all saints to her way of thinking. That's why when it came time for me to graduate from eighth grade at St. Nicholas of Bari, my mother would not hear of me going to any public high school, whether it was down Fordham Road to Teddy Roosevelt or all the way to the High School of Printing in Manhattan. My father, God bless him, wouldn't hear of sending me to any school run by any of those "sick perverts" and was holding out for public education. As September approached, the three of us were at an impasse as regards my future.

The solution came by way of my Aunt Florence, who was even crazier about the Church than my mom. She had always wanted to be a nun although for some reason or other that never worked out. So she did the next best thing. She spent her life as housekeeper for the priests at St. Finbarr's. This was a real old-school parish up in the North Bronx where the immigrants liked to settle straight from Belfast, most of them probably without papers. It turns out that those greenhorns didn't feel safe sending their kids, boys or girls, out of sight of the jam-packed five story walkups where they all lived. Years ago, old Monsignor Noonan turned the top floor of his K-8 operation into a high school, or for what passed as one. And this institute of advanced learning was the only co-ed Catholic high school in the borough. It was supposed to be just for families living in the parish but thanks to my maiden aunt's powers of persuasion, the monsignor offered me a spot in the freshman class. Tuition was next to nothing, which made my father happy, and the place was run not by those perverted Brothers but by the sweet-faced Sisters of St. Joseph of Carondelet.

September came around and I was climbing on the 41 bus every morning for a trip up Webster Avenue to my new school. I was surprised that I liked the place right away, mainly because it was not much different from 8th grade. Or 6th grade, for that matter. Classes, even math, were all stuff I already knew and for the first time in my life, I was a straight A student. Another bonus: the school was so small that I made the J.V. basketball team, no problem despite my limited skills.

Ninth grade was a breeze, likewise tenth. I was just sailing along as if I had lived up in that neighborhood my whole life. I had some pals and we'd hang out in front of the candy store on Kingsbridge Road most weekends, shooting the shit, scoring some beer and what made it really great, hanging out with the local girls. With those huge families, Mom and Pop couldn't keep close track of their red-haired daughters and I learned all about making out and grabbing a few quick feels in St. Finbarr's playground. They never went too far, of course, being good Catholic girls.

The summer before 11th grade I had my first real job stocking shelves and bagging groceries which gave me a pocket full of cash when I hopped on the 41 for the first day of school. All that dough gave me a new confidence and I looked around for a girl I could put the moves on, maybe a nice little Puerto Rican chick on her innocent way to Immaculate Conception. But all I could see on the bus were some tough looking Italian girls and I didn't want any trouble with the greaseball boyfriends they were sure to have. Then I spotted the familiar green and black plaid skirt of a St. Finbarr's girl. What was she doing taking the bus? Everybody in that school but me lived in walking distance.

She seemed to be pretty plain, with blue plastic glasses, and she was all bent down, hunched over her bookbag. I watched her for maybe ten or fifteen blocks and she never took her eyes off the floor. I kept trying to think of a way to catch her eye, maybe smile to make her feel less shy. But by then we had come to the stop for St. F's, and I followed her off the bus. She walked along as if she knew the way, but I don't know how she could even see where she was going. She kept looking at the sidewalk and never once lifted her head. Poor kid, I thought to myself, she must be scared out of her mind.

Just then a couple friends called out my name and we had to go through the whole show about how was your summer, it really sucked etc. I forgot all about the shy little girl when a couple of babes from the playground showed up and pretty soon, we were all laughing it up over nothing.

There was only one homeroom per grade, the school was that small, and I was surprised to see the new girl creeping in the door after everybody else had settled down. She looked about 14 and I had figured she was a new Freshman, but she was in our year. Sister Aurelia had already started her welcoming speech about how important for college our grades were going to be when she spotted the new girl . "Won't you welcome our newest member of the Junior class, Kathleen Mazzetti. Her family has come to see the value of a truly Catholic education and that's why Kathleen is transferring to us from Theodore Roosevelt High School."

Kathleen turned bright red with all the eyes on her, but Sister Aurelia knew how to make a newcomer feel comfortable. She sat her down next to the one girl who was even shyer and plainer than her, Helen Cassidy, and told Helen to be her buddy and show her the ropes. "I'm sure you two are going to be great friends," she smiled, actually patting Kathleen on the head.

I can't say that I really noticed the new girl much for the next few days. She was in Chemistry class with me, but so was everybody else in the grade. When Helen Cassidy turned out to be even clumsier than her with the test tubes, Sister John Edmond paired me up with Kathleen as lab partner. Some of the popular girls made faces behind her back, as if they felt sorry for me having to babysit such a loser. I didn't like that at all, which made me go out of my way to be nice to Kathleen. I think she appreciated it, especially since none of the other boys gave her the time of day. She ran for the bus right after school and never hung around like I did so she didn't really make any friends.

Some mornings I would find a seat next to her on the bus and we'd get to talking about this and that. She had two little sisters and no brothers. She thought I must be lonely because I was an only child. Her mom was Irish and her father was Italian. They didn't have much money and lived in a one-bedroom on Arthur Avenue, the Bronx version of Little Italy. Her father was a janitor at Teddy Roosevelt and when she used to go there, she hated to see him having to sweep up the mess the kids left in the cafeteria, and she'd feel really sorry for him. When I asked her why she left the public high school, she clammed up.

We'd talk about other things, like what kind of music she liked, which was old Mario Lanza records of her mother's. And how she'd been taking care of her sisters every afternoon when she got home so her mother could go to her night job in the laundry at St. Barnabas Hospital.

Even though we liked to talk on the bus, I'm embarrassed now to admit that I didn't want to be seen with her around school. She just wasn't that good-looking, and I didn't want anybody to think she was my girlfriend. That's why I kind of avoided her except when there was an excuse to be together, like on the bus or as lab partners in Chem.

Just before Christmas vacation, I noticed that Kathleen was starting to look down at her feet all the time, like when she first came to St. Finbarr's. I couldn't even get her to say much of anything on the bus, which was unusual. I wondered if she was mad at me, if I had said something to hurt her feelings. She said nothing was wrong but I thought she looked scared.

Kathleen was absent when school started again after New Year. There had been a big snowstorm and a lot of the buses weren't even running. I thought maybe that was why she wasn't at school. But she didn't show up the next day or the day after that. I kept looking around on the bus each morning but no Kathleen. I did notice one older guy with slicked up Elvis-style hair who was giving me some hard looks. I had never seen him on the bus before. He was shorter than me and looked like he lifted weights.

When Kathleen didn't show up after a week, I asked Helen if she had heard from her and she acted like they weren't friends any more. "How would I know what she's doing?"

I was thinking about her in American History class, looking over at her empty seat when Sister Eloise called out my name and that of two other guys, Billy Kelly and Jimmy Costello, two real dweebs who never hung out in the playground and who you could see were on their way to being priests if the seminary would have them. "Monsignor Noonan would like to speak with you boys," said Sister Elly.

"Are we in trouble?" whispered Billy to Jimmy once we were out in the hallway headed for the stairs.

"What do I have in common with these two altar boys?" is what I asked myself.

"Sit down," said the Monsignor, putting out his cigar and pointing to three chairs he had lined up in front of his desk. I kept looking over his head at a big picture of the Madonna breast feeding the Baby Jesus.

"I'm going to tell you something in strictest confidence, gentlemen." He looked slowly from one to another of us, probably trying to remember the sins we had told him in the privacy of the confessional booth. "Strictest confidence. That means you must never reveal anything of what I am about to tell you. Are you willing to accept this kind of responsibility?"

We nodded, and he nodded back. "You all know the new girl, Kathleen Mazzetti?" We continued to nod.

"She's a very nice girl. Would you agree?" We agreed.

"Would you say that she is a girl of good character?"

"I don't really know her, Monsignor," said Billy Kelly.

"Neither do I, Monsignor," chimed in Jimmy Costello.

"I know her," I told him. "Kathleen is a very good person. Who's saying she isn't?"

I could see that the Monsignor didn't like my tone. But I wasn't going to let anybody run her down. What was he trying to do? Expel her just because she was shy and didn't have any friends to speak up for her?

"I'm happy to hear you say that, young man." The Monsignor looked at the other two and shook his head slightly, as if he had found his favorite altar boys to be lacking on this occasion. "Would you say she's a chaste girl?"

"Chaste?" What was he getting at?

"Pure. Not promiscuous. Not one to bestow her favors freely."

"If you mean is she a good girl, I am sure she is. She doesn't hang around with boys at all. She rushes home every afternoon to watch her little sisters."

The Monsignor seemed to be pleased. "That means that you can be an excellent character reference for her, if it comes to that. All three of you, I suppose, but you will do the talking, Hanlon."

"Character reference?" I couldn't figure this out. Was somebody going around saying Kathleen was a slut?

"Let me explain the situation. Kathleen came to us because she was being harassed by a young man at the public high school, a certain John Rovazzi. He was older, already 19 and doing a second year as a Senior when she was in 9th grade. He started following her around and trying to, well, molest her. She rebuffed his advances. Do you follow me so far?"

"Yes, I think we do, Monsignor," I answered for the two dummies. "Some guy was bothering her so she came to St. Finbarr's to get away from him."

"Exactly." I could see that the Monsignor was relieved not to have to get into every detail. I was angry already at this creep who was picking on such a shy, innocent little girl.

"But transferring to another school did not end the

problem. The Rovazzi boy showed up here after school and began to harass her again. He followed her to the bus and he tried to sit next to her. He followed her home. He began to stand outside her family's apartment and call out things, obscene things."

"Did this start right before Christmas, Monsignor?"

"How did you know that, Hanlon?"

"She started acting funny," I tried to explain. "I see her on the bus and sometimes we talk. But just before Christmas, she started to look scared."

"I am sure she is afraid," said the Monsignor, "and that's why I need you gentlemen to be ready to stand up and speak about her good character. Are you willing to do that in court?"

The other two nodded uncertainly and I said that I definitely would.

"On Monday we will drive down to the courthouse on 161st street to be present at a hearing. Kathleen's parents are seeking an order of protection against the Rovazzi boy and you may be called upon to state that she is not the kind of girl who encourages improper attentions. Are you willing to stand up and say that?"

"Of course," I told the Monsignor.

Well, as it happened, we weren't called on to say anything. The whole proceeding was over in about five minutes when Rovazzi agreed to stay away from Kathleen and her family. He had a lawyer who did most of the talking for him. Kathleen had only her father, a beat-down looking little man who didn't speak loudly enough for me to hear a word that he said. Kathleen answered each of the questions the judge asked her with yes or no. She never looked up but I was sure she knew I was there in the back of the courtroom.

When Rovazzi turned to leave with his slick-looking father, he was smirking at Kathleen as if he had just pulled a fast one. He was the same stocky guy with the Elvis hair I had seen on the bus earlier that week.

The two altar boys didn't notice a thing but as we were riding back uptown in the Monsignor's Buick, I told him that I didn't trust Rovazzi. "Did you see how he was looking at Kathleen after it was all over?"

"I wouldn't worry about it, Hanlon," the Monsignor reassured me. "Young Rovazzi been put on notice that if he violates the order of protection, he can be sent to jail. That will keep him on the straight and narrow. I have learned that his father is a highly respected businessman and he will make sure that his son does nothing further to bring discredit on the family."

"I hope so, Monsignor."

After that, it seemed that Kathleen was deliberately avoiding me. She was on the same bus again but when I sat next to her, she didn't want to say much. She never liked to be the center of attention and the Rovazzi business must have been very embarrassing for her, especially after rumors circulated about the harassment and the court hearing. I kept my promise to the Monsignor and never said a word but those altar boys Kelly and Costello made sure they got a lot of mileage out of their non-role in the case. Within a couple days, everybody was talking about Kathleen and "her crazy boyfriend," especially the popular girls who loved to gossip, anyway.

A couple weeks after that, I noticed that Kathleen wasn't on the bus but when I came into homeroom, there she was. "I guess you caught the early bus today?" I smiled at her and I didn't care what anybody thought about me being friendly to her.

"Not exactly," she whispered back. "I'm staying with my aunt up here now."

Even though she was living only a couple blocks from school, Kathleen still hurried away right after the three o'clock bell. I started sitting next to her at lunch because she was so alone and I tried to get her to talk. "Why don't you hang out after school sometime? You could watch basketball practice and see how bad I am. I hardly ever make a basket."

"Maybe some time."

"What else do you have to do, anyway? You don't have to watch your little sisters anymore, do you?"

"My mother had to quit her job because of me." She started to cry a little bit. "Because I can't watch them."

A couple days after that, I ran to catch up as she hurried off and walked her to her aunt's apartment building. I started to do that nearly every day and I could tell that she didn't mind.

"I could protect you if that bastard Rovazzi shows up," I told her, which was probably a stupid thing to say.

"I'm afraid," she told me. "I'm afraid all the time."

"What can he do? Bullies like him are always punks if somebody stands up to them."

"My father stood up to him when he came to our house looking for me and Johnny punched him in the face."

"When was this? Was this after you got the order of protection?"

"Last week." She was crying again and I felt bad for making her cry.

"Come on, don't cry," I told her. "Your father can go to the court now and they'll put Rovazzi in jail. That's what an order of protection means. You're protected by the law now."

"My father said he won't go to the police."

"But why not?"

"He's afraid Johnny's father will do something even worse if he makes more trouble.'

"What's that punk's father got to do with it?"

"He's a big man in our neighborhood. He's got connections and my father said he could really hurt us, even my little sisters, if we make any trouble for his son."

"Is he in the Mafia or something?" I tried to make a joke of it. "Who is he? Don Corleone?"

"Something like that."

This conversation really upset Kathleen so I dropped the Rovazzi subject. I was sure she must be exaggerating. Her father was probably scared of his own shadow. He looked like that kind of guy.

Time went by and everything seemed to be more or less okay with Kathleen. I made the baseball team that spring and was busy with practice and games over in Van Cortlandt Park so I wasn't walking her home to her aunt's place. I never even knew when Rovazzi found out where she was staying.

Later on, Kathleen told me he would pound on her aunt's door every night, sometimes in the middle of the night, and run away before anybody opened the door. And he would call over and over and hang up without saying anything.

I could see how this was shaking up Kathleen long before she broke down and told me what was happening. Baseball season had ended and I wanted to walk her home again like I had been doing in the winter but she told me not to.

"Why not? I thought you liked to kid around with me."

"I do. That's not it."

"Then why do you mind if I walk along with you? It's only a couple blocks."

"I don't want him to hurt you," she whispered in a low voice even though we were out in front of the school and nobody else was nearby.

"Who?"

When she wouldn't answer, I guessed "Rovazzi?"

She nodded, looking around as if he might suddenly appear.

"Has he been up here bothering you?"

That's when she told me about the crank calls and the knocks on the door.

"Maybe it's not him."

"I know it is."

"Have you seen him?"

"No, but I know he's around. I know he's watching me all the time."

Now she had me getting paranoid and I looked up and down to the street to see if I could spot the creep.

"What can I do?"

"Just stay away from me. That's what I want you to do."

I reached out to touch her hand. She pulled back as if she were burnt and took off running up the street. I wasn't going to run after her, that would be crazy, so I just watched her go. I wondered if she was right about Rovazzi harassing her again or if he had just gotten so scared that she was imagining things.

The only time she'd let me talk to her was in Chem Lab or the lunchroom, never outside the school. She told me again that she didn't want him to hurt me, and he would if he thought we were going out together.

"But we're not going out. We're just friends, right? A boy and girl can be friends, can't they?"

"He wouldn't know anything about that. He'd be insanely jealous if he saw you walking with me."

"How did you ever get mixed up with a jerk like that? Why does he keep picking on you?" I guess maybe unconsciously I was absorbing some of the gossip the popular girls were spreading about Kathleen, how she used to be hot and heavy with Rovazzi and that he went crazy when she stopped putting out for him.

"That's why I don't put out for any boy," I overheard Sharon Murphy whisper to Karen Brennan in English class. "It makes them crazy when you stop."

"Besides," Karen had told her. "It's a mortal sin and you might get pregnant."

"That, too," agreed her friend. "And did you hear about how Little Miss Priss was pregnant with Rovazzi's baby and she got rid of it and that's what really made him crazy?"

"You're just making that up."

"I am not! I heard it from somebody who really knows!"

That's how the popular girls talked about Kathleen and it made me sick. It even made me stop hanging around the playground on weekends and trying to put the make on any of them. Not that they were that interested in such kid stuff, any more, having set their sights on the kind of boys who went to Xavier or Regis.

What Kathleen finally did get around to telling me about Rovazzi was the exact opposite of all that gossip they were spreading about her

She said that in the summer after 8th grade she took her sisters on the bus to Orchard Beach and they were just sitting there playing with their pails and shovels when Rovazzi came by and offered to help the kids build the greatest sandcastle in the world. He made the little girls laugh and Kathleen said that he didn't seem like a bad person. He asked what high school she went to and when she said she was starting at Teddy Roosevelt, he said he went there and would look out for her. "I'll be like your big brother," he told her and she didn't mind the idea of having a friend at a school which had the reputation of being full of gangs and drugs.

As soon as she showed up, Rovazzi started acting like he was her boyfriend. He'd catch up with her in the halls between classes and put his arm around her. He'd try to push her up against the lockers and kiss her. She had never kissed a boy and I guess his aggressiveness made her feel flattered and scared at the same time.

But when he followed her into the girls room, forced her into a stall and tried to pull down her pants, she was just scared and not flattered any more. If some older girls had not come into the bathroom just then, he probably would have raped her.

This continued for two years, off and on. There were long stretches when Rovazzi switched his focus to some other poor girl but he always came back to bothering Kathleen. He took to making fun of her father whenever he was mopping up or emptying waste baskets. He'd wait outside her classes and follow her to the next one, trying to talk to her or put his arm around her.

"Did you tell anybody?" I asked her.

"I told my English teacher, Miss Lesser. She was really nice even though I never participated in discussions. She had seen how nervous I got when Johnny showed up after class. She asked if he was stalking me and I said he only kept following me around.

"That's what stalking is." Miss Lesser told me. "You don't have to put up with that. You can go to the Dean and he'll make him stop."

She even took me to the Dean, Mr. Cohen. I told him all about Johnny and he said that's how guys are and I didn't have to be so scared around boys. "But I'll talk to him," he said.

"Did that help?"

"Not for very long. Johnny stayed away for a couple weeks but then he was back and he started following me home telling me he loved me and couldn't live without me."

"So this went on all year?"

"And all the next year, too, even though he had finally gotten his diploma by then and wasn't in the school anymore. He'd wait outside and try to catch me as I was leaving but Teddy Roosevelt has a lot of exits and I was usually able to sneak out without him seeing me."

"That's when you decided to transfer to St. Finbarr's?"

"Yes. My Mom went to the priest at our parish and asked him to help me find another school where I'd be safe. I wanted to go to Mount St. Ursula but they didn't accept transfers. Finally, he told us about St. Finbarr's and my Mom said I could go if I would watch my sisters so she could get a job. That's the only way we could afford the tuition. Now that she can't work, I'm afraid I won't be able to stay here and I'll have to go back to Teddy Roosevelt. Or maybe I can go to Walton. That's the only public school just for girls."

"Is he still knocking on your aunt's door and making crank calls?"

Kathleen nodded.

"Have you seen him? Has he tried to bother you?"

She nodded again. I was thinking about whether I could take Rovazzi in a fair fight but he looked pretty strong. I wondered if maybe I could sucker punch him when he was looking the other way. But all that was just fantasy and I knew it.

"He must know you don't like him. Why doesn't he give up?"

"There's something wrong with him. There has to be something wrong with him."

She couldn't make sense of him any more than I could. She didn't know what she could do to make him stop and I sure didn't have any idea either.

"If you can think of anything I could do, you have to tell me." That's what I said to her.

"You could kill him." Kathleen looked up at me, her blue eyes matching her blue plastic glasses. "You could kill him. That's the only way to make him stop."

"You're joking, right?"

"Not really" was her answer. She was a pretty small girl but at that moment she scared the hell out of me. After a minute or two, we both laughed and brushed it off as a joke.

"We could find out where he eats and poison his lunch."

"Or we could tamper with the brakes on the big Oldsmobile his father gave him," she smiled.

"We could lure him into the subway and push him in front of a train," I laughed.

Her face suddenly became as serious as anybody's I

ever saw. "Now that's a plan that just might work."

Like I said, she was starting to scare me. She wasn't kidding about wanting to kill this guy. I believed her when she said that was the only way to stop him, especially after what happened that June.

It was the next to the last day of school when Kathleen failed to show up in class. I kept thinking about her all day and as soon as the bell rang, I ran over to her aunt's build-ing, climbed up to the fourth floor and knocked on the door. At first nobody answered but I could hear people moving around inside.

"There's somebody at the door. Maybe it's the police," I heard a woman say. I guessed she was Kathleen's aunt.

"You know it's not the cops." Can that be Rovazzi, I asked myself. I knocked again.

"I have to answer the door."

"You stay sitting right where you are, bitch."

I knocked again, my heart pounding.

"Johnny, you have to go now or you'll get in trouble." That was Kathleen's voice! What was he doing in the apartment? How did he get in? Had he hurt her?

The door opened suddenly and I was face to face with him.

"Who the fuck are you? Get the fuck out of here."

I didn't move. I was probably paralyzed with fear but I guess he couldn't see that. I wasn't able to say a word even if I wanted to.

"I asked you who the fuck you are!"

At that point Rovazzi moved toward me, away from the open door and Kathleen was through it in a flash running like crazy down the stairs. I was blocking Rovazzi and he pushed me out the way like I was a toothpick and took off after her. Her aunt was in the doorway now, screaming somebody help us, he's going to kill us.

I ran after Rovazzi and found him in the street, looking every which way. It turned out Kathleen had ducked into an apartment on the second floor just when a lady she knew opened the door to see what was going on. She was up there in a total panic and I was on the building's stoop looking to see where she'd gone.

Kathleen's aunt had opened her window and yelled down at him. "I've called the cops on you, you fucking asshole!"

Rovazzi saw me looking at him and had already taken a few steps in my direction when he stopped to look up at the fourth-floor window where the aunt was yelling her head off.

I distinctly heard him say "I'll kill you, too" before he took off and disappeared around the corner.

By the time the cops arrived a half hour later, I was in the aunt's kitchen and knew the whole story. Rovazzi had showed up early that morning and forced his way into the apartment. He told them he would kill both of them if they tried to scream for help or get away. He said could strangle them with his bare hands and nobody would ever know who did it.

"He said we were going to calmly talk about our relationship and work through all our problems," Kathleen said to me. "That's what he said we were going to do. He said he didn't want to have to kill anybody but he would if I didn't listen to reason."

"It must have been terrible. He was here all day?"

"He just kept talking, saying the same thing over and over."

"Kathy was wonderful," her aunt said, hugging her.

"She managed to keep her head, I don't know how. When he started to get agitated, she said that she was still so young and that maybe things would work out for them later when she finished college."

"I didn't mean any of it." She turned to me, her eyes as cold as death. "I hate him."

She was scaring me again because I knew what she was thinking. "I know but at least you were able to fool him into thinking he had a chance. That was the only thing you could do."

"The problem is that now he really believes I'll marry him some day. He might do anything once he realizes how I lied to him, how I told him all kinds of lies just to keep him from killing us." She started to break down and her aunt put her arms around her again.

"You don't ever have to worry about him again, honey," her aunt told her. "When we tell the cops how he came here and held us captive, they'll put him away for life. That's kidnapping. There's the Lindbergh law that says you can even get the electric chair for kidnapping someone."

Well, as it turns out, nobody got the chair. In fact, the cops acted as if I were suspect number one.

"And who are you?" the taller one asked me after Kathleen and her aunt had told them what happened. "Are you the other boyfriend in this little teenage triangle?"

"I'm Kathleen's friend." I think I was starting to stutter, the way they were looking at me. "From school. I'm in Kathleen's class at St. Finbarr's."

"So you and this other character are fighting over the girl, is that it?" The shorter cop looked skeptically at Kathleen, as if amazed that a girl who looked like her could bring out the beast in anybody.

"And how do you know this other guy, what's his name, Renzulli?"

"Rovazzi." Kathleen's voice was surprisingly strong, unlike mine. "His name is John Rovazzi and he's been harassing me for the past three years."

"I'll ask again," said the tall cop. "You know this joker here from school, right? How do you know the other one, Rovazzi?"

"He was at Teddy Roosevelt when I went there."

"So, you've gone out with both these guys, one at TR and one up here at St. Finn's, is that the story?"

"I have not gone out with either of them but Paul Hanlon is a good friend and John Rovazzi has threatened to kill me and my aunt. He held us captive here and threatened to kill us unless we listened to him."

"Listen to him? You mean all he wanted was to have a talk with you? He didn't try to rape either of you, did he? Did he hit you?"

"He threatened to kill us. What part of that can't you understand?" Her aunt was beginning to lose her temper with these two and I couldn't blame her.

"Calm down, lady," said the short cop. "Just tell me, did he display a weapon? A gun or a knife?"

"He said he would fucking strangle us."

"Getting excited isn't helping your case, lady. And you'd better mind your language."

Kathleen stood up and put her arm around her aunt's waist. "Officer, just tell us what we can do now."

"Now?"

"Yes, what can we do now to protect ourselves?"

"Well, we'll make a full report and I expect a detective may want to talk to you. And to Mr. Rovazzi, of course." Then he remembered I was there, too. "I'll need to get all your information, you included. The detective will probably want to talk with you since you're a….a witness, I guess, if nothing more."

"When will the detective do this?"

"Well, they're swamped with serious cases but something like this, a domestic dispute, I'd say you should hear from the detective in a week or so. He'll call first to set up a time to talk."

"A week?" That little Kathleen was like steel now. "In a week he could kill us all, don't you understand that?"

"Just don't get all worked up over this and everything will be fine, you'll see." The tall cop tried a kind of fake smile to provide some reassurance but none of us were buying it.

"We see this kind of thing all the time," the short cop said as they headed for the door. "People get steamed up and then it all blows over."

Kathleen ran after them and leaned over the stairwell as they went clomping down to the third floor. "I forgot to tell you I have an order of protection against him. Doesn't that count for anything?'

"We'll add it to the report," one of the cops called back. "Just let us know if there's any more problems.

After the cops had gone, and with all the stress of being held prisoner, the aunt was a wreck and needed a few quick shots from a bottle of the Four Roses she kept under the sink. When she dozed off on the couch, Kathleen and I sat down at the kitchen table to talk things out.

"The cops are not going to do anything" was the first thing she said.

"That's the way it looks but maybe…"

"Johnny thinks I love him now. I had to convince him of that or he would have killed us. He's going to be back as soon as he thinks it's safe."

"Then we have to get out of here before he does."

We managed to rouse the aunt into some kind of groggy wakefulness and guided her down the stairs to her friend's apartment where she immediately passed out.

"Don't let her go home, no matter what you do," Kathleen told the friend. When we got down to the street, Rovazzi was nowhere in sight and we just walked as fast as we could out of the neighborhood. We ended up sitting on a marble bench on the edge of Woodlawn Cemetery, a place not even Rovazzi would think to look for us.

"I wish Johnny were under one of those gravestones." Kathleen was resting her head on my shoulder. "Would you kiss me please?"

I kissed her, a nice warm kiss. She smiled back at me. "My first kiss, just the way I imagined it."

"Really? I'm glad."

"Unless I count Rovazzi putting his ugly mouth all over me, which I don't."

"He doesn't count."

"He doesn't count for shit! He isn't worth shit!"

After we kissed again, and it was even better this time, Kathleen leaned her head back on my shoulder and asked me a question: "Do you remember that idea you had?"

"What idea was that?"

"About pushing Johnny in front of a train."

"But I was only …"

"I know you weren't really serious then but now…"

"Now?"

"Now you know he'll kill me if I don't let him fuck me." I had never heard such language from Kathleen. It made me realize how serious how she was, if I didn't know that already.

"You don't want him to fuck me, do you?"

"Of course not."

He said he would kill me, too, but I didn't mention that to Kathleen. If I was going to do something, I was going to do it for her and not for myself. "You're serious, aren't you?"

"We don't really have any other choice. If I run away, he'll probably kill my whole family, even my little sisters."

"You really and truly think he's capable of that? Maybe he's just making threats to get you to do what he wants."

"His grandfather was in prison for twenty years for killing a man in Brooklyn."

"Really?"

"Johnny said his father sent him out to Texas to stay with the grandfather last month, to get him away from me. He was supposed to stay out there but he said he couldn't live without me so he came back after only a week. He told me he bought a gun when he was in Texas and he would use it to commit suicide after he killed me. He said he didn't want to kill me but he would if he had to."

"Did you see the gun?"

"What does that matter?" She was angry now. "Are you going to help me or do I have to do this all by myself?"

"No, no." I kissed her again. "I'll help you."

"Good. Let's make a plan. Give me some paper and we'll write it all out so we won't make any mistakes."

I had been carrying my schoolbag all this while and I took out my looseleaf and a pen. Kathleen was all business as she started to write. "First, we need a quiet subway stop where there won't be witnesses. I'll tell him I've run away from home and want to be with him forever." She wrote that down.

"I can't live without you. That's what I'll tell him. I'll say that he doesn't come to me, I will kill myself."

"Is he likely to believe that?"

"Yes, because that's the way he thinks, like a fucking psycho. I can think like a fucking psycho too when I have to. He'll believe me."

"Okay, so where will you meet him?"

"The best place would be the 182nd Street stop on the D Train. I'll tell him I've run away from home and I want to be far away from the neighborhood where somebody might see me and tell my parents. I'll say we have to meet really late because then there'll be fewer people in the station."

"But won't he want to know why you need to meet him in a subway station? Like are you taking the train somewhere?"

Kathleen stopped to think, chewing on the pen. "I've got it! I'll say I want him to take me to the midnight show at the Astor down in Greenwich Village. That's where they have the Rocky Horror Picture Show. I've always wanted to go there so I can be believable when I tell him about it. People dress up in zombie costumes and act really crazy. He's probably heard about it, too."

"You won't really go to the show with him, will you?"

"No, of course not. You'll be waiting, hidden somewhere, and I'll distract him just as the train starts coming in. I'll jump back away from him and you give him a good, strong shove and over he goes."

"It'll be a real mess."

"I won't look at him. We'll run out of there as fast as we can and I'll never have to think about him again."

"What if I can't get the chance to push him off the platform? What if he's grabbing onto you and I can't risk pushing him without him pulling you onto the tracks?"

Kathleen stopped to think again. "Well, you have to do it, that's all. I'm depending on you to save my life."

"What if he's not standing in the right place for me to push him?"

"You're worrying too much." She put her arms around me. "We can do it. Even if somehow you miss the first chance, I'll go to the show with him and we'll come back to the same station and you'll get a second chance. You really shouldn't need more than two opportunities for this, if you really want to help me."

I must have looked like I was losing my nerve.

"Do you really want to save my life or not?"

"Of course, I do! Of course, I'll do it!"

The first part of our plan didn't go as smoothly as Kathleen had expected. She had written a whole script of what she wanted to tell Rovazzi and I held the paper for her as she dialed a payphone at the 205th Street station. His mother said he wasn't home. Kathleen didn't believe her and called again, hoping Rovazzi would pick up this time. His mobbed-up father answered that time and he wanted to know who was this girl calling his son. Kathleen made up a name. He said he never heard of her and hung up.

"Johnny's probably out looking for me. I have to go where he can find me."

"That's too dangerous. How can I protect you if he pulls out that gun and suddenly shoots you?"

"I'll just lay this load of bullshit on him as soon as I see him." She waved the script at me.

"You can't exactly read all that stuff to him."

"Of course not! I'll memorize it on the way downtown. You'll see. I'm a good actress. I can make him believe me."

"Maybe you'll become an actress when you grow up."

"Maybe. If I get the chance to grow up, that is."

We hopped on the D Train and took it to 182nd to check out the station. It looked good. There was a column I could hide behind and watch him coming down the stairs. Kathleen said she would go up to him and start talking so he wouldn't see me sneaking up on him. Then I'd get my chance.

We took the train back up to Fordham Road. "I'll walk a block ahead so he won't see that we're together, if he's around. You follow me from the other side of the street."

"Okay, sure thing," I said, trying to sound confident.

"I'll go to Teibout Avenue where he lives and wander around in front of his house until he sees me."

It was getting dark as we set off, and there were so many people on Fordham Road shopping or going home from work that I kept losing sight of her. When she turned down Tiebout, I dropped back a couple more blocks. We weren't by his house very long before a big yellow Olds suddenly screeched to a halt before quickly backing halfway up the street.

I couldn't hear what Kathleen was saying to Rovazzi. She was leaning into the passenger side window. He must have wanted her to get into the car. I kept praying she wouldn't do that because he would immediately drive her somewhere deserted where he could rape her, and she'd have to go along and pretend she liked it. I knew she was a good actress, but I didn't think even she could pull off that much acting before he figured out that she really despised him. Then he'd just kill her and dump her naked body somewhere.

I was about to shout at her to run when Rovazzi turned off the engine and got out of the car. More talking followed, none of which I could hear. He wasn't raising his voice and that was a good sign. They turned toward me and I could see they were holding hands. It made me sick but I knew she had to do it.

They were walking slowly straight toward me, heading back toward Fordham Road. Fortunately, somebody came out of an apartment building just then and I was able to duck into the lobby before the door clicked shut. Through the smudged glass I watched the two of them pass by, all smiles.

I stayed a block back on the other side of the street. She must have convinced him to take her to the Rocky Horror Show and I gave her a lot of credit for persuading him to go by subway. I'm sure he would have preferred to show off in the big new car his daddy gave him.

When they reached the Grand Concourse, they headed down into the subway. I was close behind but I knew our plan couldn't work at such a busy station. To tell you the truth, I was a little relieved that she couldn't get him to go to the deserted station at 182nd where I would have to do something I really didn't want to do.

But I told myself I would do it if I had to.

I followed them down the steps and dropped a token in the turnstile. For a minute I thought they had caught the previous train but then I spotted them way down at the far end of the platform, his hands all over her. A train came roaring into the station and they were on it before I was anywhere near them. I jumped into another car just as the doors wheezed shut behind me.

When they got out at West 4th, I was right behind them. Kathleen looked back once and I know she saw me. Following the same system as before, I stayed a block or two behind until they came to the theater. When they went inside, I stationed myself across the street and waited. I didn't even want to think about what Kathleen had to do in that dark theater to keep him convinced that she was crazy about him.

I was nearly asleep, leaning on a garbage can, when the crowd came dancing out of the theater. And I mean dancing, literally. They were all dressed up as if it were Halloween and most of them seemed pretty high. After they had cleared out, I saw no sign of Kathleen and Rovazzi so I took a chance they'd head toward the nearest subway, which was Astor Street. And there they were, grabbing onto each other and kissing furiously in the middle of the sidewalk, with people having to walk around them. "Get a room!" said one wise guy.

Kathleen was doing what she had to do. And I was going to do what I had to do. Finally, the lip-lock ended and they were down the subway steps. I was out of tokens and had to take a chance hopping the turnstile or I would have lost them. Fortunately, no transit cops were lurking nearby

The kissing scene had delayed them long enough for

the movie crowd to have already caught a train and the station was completely empty. The guy in the token booth had no clear view to see what was happening down near the tracks.

They were still smooching away and Rovazzi doubtless had visions of getting Kathleen into bed, or at least on her back, somewhere soon. He was far too distracted to see me coming. The problem was that he had his arms wrapped like tentacles around Kathleen. He was right near the edge of the platform with his back to me.

I was getting closer and closer to them until I was just standing there out in the open with no place to hide.

"Kathleen," I said. "Is that really you all the way down here in the Village?"

"What the fuck…" Rovazzi stepped back, letting go of her and balling up his fists. "Who the fuck…" I could see right away that he remembered my face. He looked at Kathleen and then back toward me, and then her. "You fucking bitch! You fucking two-timing bitch!"

People say everything was a blur or they blacked out but I remember every second. Kathleen shouting his name, him turning, a quick push, the look in his eyes as he tried to get back on his feet, the roar of the oncoming train, the scream, us running and running.

When we reached Second Avenue, we slowed to a walk, a really slow walk nobody would notice. We held hands. We stopped and kissed like any couple in love would. Somewhere near Times Square, I even remembered to tear up our script. I can still see the little pieces of paper blowing away down Seventh Avenue.

We were sitting on a bench near Bethesda Fountain in Central Park when the sun came up, a beautiful early summer morning. The water from the fountain was sparkling. Birds were singing, something we didn't hear in the Bronx. For some reason we weren't worried about our parents yelling at us for staying out all night. We weren't even worried about getting arrested or going to jail.

Everything that we worried about that morning, about how our parents would go berserk over us being out all night or how the cops would question us about Rovazzi or whether we'd go to jail, turned out not to happen in the ways that we imagined.

About the Author

Michael Cooney has published poetry in *Badlands, Second Chance Lit, Bitter Oleander, Big Windows Review* and other journals. His short stories have appeared recently in *Sundial Magazine, Bandit Fiction* and *Cerasus* and his novella *The Witch Girl & The Wobbly* was published by Running Wild Press in 2021. He has taught in public high schools and community colleges and currently facilitates a writing workshop with the New York Writers Coalition.

The Confession

There was a very long pause before she got the second assent. The police did not sound any more thrilled with Felicity's new weapon than she was.

Don't worry, Florence thought with a sigh. *I'll try to talk her out of it at the earliest opportunity.*

Now detransformed, the two girls walked away from the park. Behind them, a police officer was gingerly pushing an enormous trolley cart that had both minions on it. One was still encased in a dripping block of ice, while the other was trailing strings of poison ivy along the ground. The police officer flinched and jerked back every time a tendril drifted near him, despite the fact that every inch of skin except for his face was covered.

"You know, if you used dandelions as your fourth seed type, it might make things more convenient for the police officers who have to collect the minions you capture," Florence hinted.

But Felicity didn't seem to notice. She was bouncing up and down excitedly. "Have you ever noticed you look different right after transforming?"

Florence was taken aback. "What do you mean?"

"Your magical girl form," Felicity said. "Your dress goes red while you're transforming, instead of pink. And your wings. They look bigger or something. As soon as you finish transforming, you look the same as always, but I kind of wonder if you're on the verge of a power-up?"

Florence digested that. She wouldn't argue that a red costume would be an improvement over pink, and her wings had gotten larger after her first power-up. All of theirs had. They'd all had tiny wings at the beginning. "When did it start?"

"I dunno," Felicity shrugged. "It just started recently — *DANIEL!*"

"Huh?" Florence asked, baffled.

"*DANIEL!*" her teammate screamed again, pointing excitedly.

Florence looked in the direction Felicity was pointing, and sure enough, there was the boy she had a stalker-crush on.

Florence just barely stopped herself from saying, "So what?" Given that her first and last boyfriend had been a Deathwave villain who'd betrayed her, she found it hard to get invested in the subject of crushes or dating nowadays.

But Felicity had no such reticence. "Oh, he's so beautiful, isn't he?" she whispered, grabbing Florence's arm. "I hope he asks me out on a date soon! I can't *wait!*"

"Felicity . . ." Florence said wearily, prying her friend's long fingernails out of her bicep, "if you really want to go out with him, why don't you ask *him?*"

Felicity stared at her as if this were a foreign concept.

"You might even tell him that you like him," Florence hinted.

Felicity gasped and put a hand to her mouth. "Oh, I couldn't! I just couldn't! What would I do if he said no? No, no, no, Daniel has to ask *me!*"

Florence let out an exasperated grunt.

The boy walking ahead of them turned around. "Huh? Did someone call me?"

Felicity's face turned approximately seven colors at once. It went everywhere from super pale to bright red to sickly green simultaneously. Since Florence was too dark-skinned to have to worry about blushing, she found the effect mildly amusing.

With a bit of impish glee, Florence said, "She did. This is my friend, Felicity."

Felicity let out a desperate choking sound.

"Oh." The guy looked at Felicity with no apparent recognition, which was astonishing given the fact that she was constantly doodling his name all over her backpack with hearts all around it. You would think the guy would've noticed by now.

Feeling even more impish, Florence added, "Felicity has the biggest cru—"

"Hi!" Felicity burst in desperately. "I — um — I — uh — oh — I — I'm Felicity!"

"Yeah, she said that," the guy said. "Why did you call me?"

Felicity's face turned red and white and green all over again. "I'm Felicity!" she gasped.

Florence had to suppress rolling her eyes.

"Okaaaaaaaay," he said, looking confused. "Well, nice to meet you, I guess."

Felicity stood there with wild eyes, stiff and straight, as the guy walked away. Florence wondered if she'd maybe gone a little too far. She hadn't meant to break her friend.

"You oka—" she began.

"Florence!!" Felicity screamed, seizing her arm. "He was glad to meet me!!"

"Hurray," Florence snorted. "Now my life is complete."

Chapter 2
The Refuge

Up above the lair so high, like a darling in the sky, Tiffany was showing off her new invention.

"And this one's name is Billy, and that one's name is Bobby, and . . ."

"Did I *ask* you to build new defenses?" Chronos glowered, leaning a ladder in between two of the four enormous cannons that now graced the top of their entryway. "Why no, I don't think I did."

"Billy can shoot cannonballs!" Tiffany effused. "Bobby can shoot bubbles! Franky can shoot pizza! Freddie can shoot freezy things! And they're all voice-activated —"

"All four cannons, self-destruct," Chronos said immediately.

Nothing happened.

Tiffany giggled. "Silly! I meant activated by *my* voice, of course!"

Of course she had. Chronos would just have to pull the cannons down the hard way. She wiggled the ladder to make sure it was stable, then started climbing up it.

"Kendra! Come admire my new cannons!" Tiffany shouted, balancing on one foot on top of one of the long metallic tubes. She held her arms out for balance, a wide grin on her face. "They're super fun and pretty and neat!"

". . . Pass," Kendra said indifferently from her position at the top of the stairs. She had been taking notes about something or another in a spiral-bound notebook for hours. Chronos would have liked to think that it was some sort of schoolwork, but alas, knowing Kendra, it was probably notes on magical girl battles.

No, make that definitely. She still hadn't managed to persuade the former magical girl pest that maybe, just maybe, it would make sense for a fifteen-year-old to go back to school.

"You wouldn't have to go back home if you don't want to face your friends or family," Chronos had griped. *"Just take a correspondence class or something! I'll pay for it!"*

"Waste of time," Kendra had retorted. *"I'm here to save the world, not pass tests."*

Chronos had taken to keeping an eye on every magical girl school in the world for signs of any flimsy excuse she could use to convince Kendra to go in undercover, but alas, none had presented themselves. She'd thought of simply lying, but despite the girl's refusal to spend any time getting an education, she wasn't stupid.

She would have loved the chance to get Tiffany out of the lair and into an elementary school even more, but that was looking even less likely. *"Other kids are all big meanies!"* had been Tiffany's indignant response to Chronos's attempt to persuade her that school would be fun. And seeing as that had been her own opinion as a kid, Chronos had found that hard to refute.

At least Tiffany had clearly gotten *some* education. The girl could read, for instance, despite having been a prisoner here since she was four years old. Apparently "Daddy" had taught her. That was the villain who had kidnapped Tiffany and made her a prisoner initially, and try as she might, Chronos had not been able to learn the man's real name. Perhaps Tiffany didn't know it. Regardless, she was glad Tiffany seemed to have been happy with that particular "master," but also more than a little wary that the child might have some serious Stockholm Syndrome.

"Freddie's freezy things are super dangerous!" Tiffany bragged. "I could make you one to kill magical girls with!"

Case in point. What ten-year-old said things like that?

"... Pass," Kendra said again.

Tiffany continued to prattle on about her brand new cannons, but Chronos's patience was at an end. She reached the top of the ladder and reached for the little girl's ankle balancing just above her head.

"Get down from there!" she ordered. "Get *down,* already!"

The little girl skipped nimbly from one cannon to the other, not seeming to notice the ten foot drop between them. "Hee heeeeeeee!" she squealed.

Argh! Chronos thought. *Exactly like that future of Lavender Mystery with —*

Hundreds of futures flickered across her mind. Chronos was taken aback, and took nearly half a second to check. There was something glaring missing from all of them. Which meant . . .

"*Why are there no futures left for Lavender Mystery?!*" Chronos shouted.

On top of the stairs, Kendra flipped a page, looking completely blasé. "She got in the way of my halo."

"I've *ordered* you not to kill anybody!" Chronos screamed.

"And I didn't. Her human life is fine."

"*Including* magical girl forms!"

"You didn't specify that."

"No more killing magical girl forms!"

"I can't guarantee that." Kendra flipped a page in her notebook, not looking up and not even looking particularly interested in the conversation.

"We could un-break Brian and brainwash them instead!" Tiffany suggested from above them. Chronos glanced up to see her lying lengthwise across a cannon.

"See?" Kendra commented. "My methods seem completely mild by comparison."

"No, they do not!" Chronos shouted.

"Ooh, that reminds me!" Tiffany squealed. "Who wants to see my blueprints for Doris the Death Ray?"

The doorbell rang.

"Suuuure," Kendra said. "I'll get that."

The Refuge

You'd think a lair would be a refuge from homicidal lunatics, Chronos fumed. *But no, I don't even feel safe with the people who are supposedly on my team!*

If all villains felt that way, she would never, ever understand why anyone chose such a bothersome way to live.

Kendra strolled through the front doorway, which had no door, but didn't need one. Thanks to the defense grid, the only people who could pass through it were her, Chronos, and Tiffany. Even insects couldn't fly in.

In the background, she heard a horrified scream. "Hey!! Don't rip it up!! Give it back!! Doriiiiiiiiiiiiiiiiis!!"

Good riddance, Kendra thought. The last thing she wanted on her missions was a weapon that somebody else could pick up and use against her.

Kendra let her eyes adjust to the bright sunshine before stepping through the barrier, noting that there were only two people standing out there, and neither of them looked particularly dangerous.

She'd half-expected to see a battalion of police or one of the magical girls she'd recently defeated, but instead, she saw two women she didn't recognize in the least. One of them was dressed in fashionable slacks under a sheer half-skirt, with a belt made from enormous chain links on top. Another wore a punkish outfit and a scarf wound around her neck and waist. They definitely weren't police or magical girls. Most likely they were fellow villains.

Once she was sure her eyes had adjusted, Kendra strode forward, summoning her spiked halo into the right hand that was hiding behind her back, just in case. "We're not interested in newsletters, we have all the allies we need, and we don't care about neighbors. That cover everything?"

"No, actually," the woman with the chain link belt said. "We're here to see my sister."

The other woman raised her pointer finger. "Name of Chronos, no fashion sense whatsoever?"

"Chronos has a family?" Kendra blurted out.

It was hard to imagine. The soothsayer was just so antisocial.

"Quite a *large* family," the woman with the chain link belt said, smiling. "My name is Rhea, and this is Minerva."

Kendra stared at them blankly. Was that supposed to mean something to her?

"From Greek mythology?" the woman said impatiently. "I mean, Minerva is the Roman name, but that's because she's technically not blood-related."

Kendra's jaw dropped. "Chronos is an *Olympian?!*"

"What did you expect, with a name like that?" the woman asked incredulously.

"I thought Olympians were named things like Zeus and Odin," Kendra protested.

For some reason, the woman looked very offended.

"Isn't that second one from a different —" the other woman began.

"*Yes.*"

Kendra had no clue what they were talking about, and she was still trying to process this. It was unbelievable. *All that time Chronos said she wasn't a villain, and she was an* Olympian? *What a liar! Was anything she told me true?*

What if she'd been manipulated?

What if her future would have been something totally different?

What if she could have stayed a magical girl?

What if the world hadn't needed her to be a villain?

Kendra was on the verge of a panic attack.

But then she remembered the details that had convinced her. Her future self's change of costume. Her future self's change of hairstyle. Both things she had imagined but never told anyone she was planning. The Magical Girl Union, which nobody had known she was serious about starting. The catchphrase echoing down through her future years: "To protect world peace!"

Kendra shuddered, shoving the thought away. No. She hadn't been mistaken. Everything she had done had been necessary.

". . . see my sister, please?" the woman with the chain link belt was saying.

Kendra shook herself. "I'll have to ask her," she said briskly. "Hey, Chronos —" she called back over her shoulder.

But footsteps were already pounding up the stairs. Chronos exploded through the barrier.

"Rhea, get out of here!" she shouted. "You're not welcome!"

"I'm pleased to see you too," the dark-haired woman said dryly.

"*Get out!*" Chronos shouted, pointing fiercely away.

"No, I don't think I will," the woman said. "We need to have a little chat, my baby sister. Besides, I brought you presents."

"So did the Greeks at Troy," Chronos muttered.

Rhea beamed.

"I am not going to have a conversation with you," Chronos snapped. "I'm not going to talk to you. You're certainly not going to get inside my lair. So just drive away, and —"

"Ooh, do we have visitors?" a voice squealed from above them. "I'll deactivate Davie! BREAK IT!"

The protective barrier made by the defense grid instantly vanished.

For a moment, Chronos looked too stunned to move. For some reason, Rhea did too.

"Who the *heck?*" Rhea screamed. "Is there another person living in there?!"

"Does your sister have more than one defector?" the other woman asked.

"How should I know?!" The dark-haired woman looked on the verge of hyperventilating. "She could have an army of people in there!"

"That's right," Chronos said with satisfaction. "There's an entire army in there waiting for you —"

But Rhea had already put her hands together and was rapidly flicking through every room inside the lair.

"How many?" Minerva asked.

"Just one," Rhea said. "Or just one a second ago." She glanced up at her sister.

"Yes, well, there are a whole bunch waiting to teleport in —" Chronos began, clearly trying to salvage the situation.

"She has the teleport watch, so you clearly don't have anyone waiting to teleport in," Rhea said, pointing at Kendra. "I suppose it's possible that she's prepared to teleport and grab reinforcements, but in that case, I doubt that you would have her standing right next to me within arm's reach —"

Kendra shoved her left hand defensively behind her back.

Rhea laughed. "Oh, I'm not going to steal the watch! I have much better toys of my own. Ones that coordinate with outfits, rather than clashing. That thing is hideously ugly."

Kendra made an involuntary face. The dark-haired woman wasn't wrong. It wasn't so much that the watch was ugly, per se, but it was decades out of fashion, and it looked like it belonged on the wrist of a businessman instead of a villain. That was why she didn't wear it when she went on missions. She tucked it into her belt instead. Sure, it might be useful in combat, but she didn't want to rely on it for anything but transportation, and she hated the idea of ruining the cool look of her villain outfit.

"Oh, did you know that I designed your costume?" the dark-haired woman broke in. "You might have heard of me. Rhea Korstanos."

Kendra's mouth fell open. "*You're* Rhea Korstanos?"

The woman smiled. "The same."

Kendra turned to look at Chronos. "*You're* related to Rhea Korstanos? *You?*"

"Unfortunately," Chronos muttered.

"I find it hard to believe myself," the woman chuckled. "Her taste in fashion is appalling, isn't it?"

"It's nonexistent," Kendra shot back.

Rhea sighed. "I've tried to educate her, you know."

"She doesn't even own an iron."

"Why would I need an iron?!"

"Because your clothes are always wrinkled!" Kendra shouted.

Rhea moved forward and put a friendly hand on Kendra's shoulder. "I'm so glad you're working with her. I think you'll be a good influence. Can I task you with ensuring that she sometimes dresses appropriately?"

"No," Chronos snorted.

"Absolutely," Kendra said, nodding.

The oracle looked extremely disgruntled.

"Now," Rhea said, clearing her throat delicately, "about why we're here —"

"Oh, speaking of which," Kendra said sharply, eyeing Chronos, "'Not all born mages are villains,' you said. 'I'm not a villain,' you said. 'Why are you so quick to judge my people, and so quick to praise yours?' you said. And you were an *Olympian?*"

"It's *true!*" Chronos said, hunching her shoulders. "Stop looking at me!"

"A-hem," Rhea said, looking a trifle annoyed at the interruption. She held up a zippered bag that had been resting by her feet. "Well, we've come to bring you a special gift —"

"Accessories!" the woman beside her enthused, unzipping it and pulling out several handfuls. "Necklaces . . . bracelets . . . buckles . . ."

Kendra's eyes fell lustfully on half a dozen black leather straps with buckles that were trapezoidal-shaped, just like the belt of her villain outfit. She wasn't sure where she would put them yet, but the costume definitely needed those.

"We don't care," Chronos said rudely. "We don't trust anything you bring. Now, if you'd just pick them up and clear out —"

"Which ones are for me?! Which ones are for me?!" Tiffany shouted, running through the doorway.

Rhea looked extremely taken aback. "Er . . . I didn't actually know you existed, so I don't have anything meant for a child your age . . ."

"*Noooooooooo!*" Tiffany howled.

Rhea placed her hands on the other woman's shoulders. "Tell you what: Minerva here will make you something!"

"I *will?*" the punkish woman asked skeptically.

"You will." Rhea's smile was like iron.

"I will," the woman muttered.

Either an employee or a minion, Kendra surmised.

"Can she make super pretty things?" Tiffany asked excitedly.

"Of course," Rhea beamed. "In fact, I'll even let you design it. Just draw it, take her inside, and she'll bring it into reality!"

"I'll go get my crayons!" Tiffany cried, racing back to the lair.

Kendra eyed the bag of accessories. She wanted those buckles. She needed those buckles. She needed those buckles right now.

"Feel free to choose whatever you want," Rhea said, smiling. "Both for your outfit and for my baby sister's."

"Cool," Kendra said, trying to seem barely interested. "My costume needs more accessories."

Chronos bolted for the doorway, and Rhea reached out and snagged her sleeve.

"...While my sister and I have a heart-to-heart chat."

Kendra casually reached for the bag and pulled out a few necklaces, several bracelets, a pair of earrings, and all of the straps with buckles, as if they were only an afterthought.

"Come! Let's go give you a makeover!" Rhea said cheerfully, pushing her sister towards the doorway.

"Just *go away!*" Chronos shouted.

As they reached the unbarriered doorway, Rhea stopped and glanced over her shoulder at her minion, who was still hanging back. The woman had the air of one who was hoping her boss would forget to make her do an unpleasant task.

"You *will*," Rhea repeated.

"I'm asking for *two* days off next week," the minion muttered, trudging after Tiffany.

Chronos had no idea why her sister was here, but she was certain about one thing: it was not to have a heart-to-heart chat.

"Do you have a brush anywhere?" Rhea asked brightly.

"No," Chronos said immediately.

But Rhea snapped her fingers, summoned up an image of where the bathrooms had been a few minutes ago, flicked through each of them until she found a brush in one of the drawers, and headed straight for the nearest bathroom.

Before Chronos could escape to her bedroom and lock the door, Rhea reappeared with the offending implement in her hand.

"I suppose you didn't know where it was because it's such a foreign object," she said cheerfully. "Have you *ever* brushed your hair more frequently than once a decade?"

Chronos glowered at her.

Rhea moved forward and attacked her hair. Chronos tried to shove her off, but to no avail.

"Show me a tour of your new place!" Rhea ordered.

Chronos snorted. That was certainly not going to happen.

"Let me see," Rhea said, her hands still moving busily through Chronos's hair despite her best attempts to shove them away. "I see you have a bedroom, enormous dungeons, a kitchen that's woefully understocked . . ."

She was going to give herself a tour if Chronos didn't stop her, it seemed.

"Let's go to the plotting room," Chronos grunted. There was nothing in there that she minded Rhea investigating closely.

She stormed down the stairs, trying to ignore how satisfied her sister looked as she followed her. When they got to the plotting room, Chronos flopped into a chair and sat there sulking while the brush continued attacking her hair.

"I'm so happy to be here to visit," Rhea said from behind her, shoving the brush through the many tangles. "It's been so long since we've had time to catch up. It seems you have two teammates! When did the other one get here?"

"I know perfectly well what you just did," Chronos grated. "You distracted them both so you could have time with me alone. So? Would you please explain why you're really here?"

Rhea gasped from behind her. "I'm shocked that you'd accuse me of duplicity! I'm *scandalized!* I'm —"

Chronos snorted. She didn't turn around. "Rhea."

"Fine." With a sudden jerk, she felt herself grabbed upward, with an arm wrapped tightly around her neck. "I want to know why you've been betraying the family."

Chapter 3
The Peril

She choked and gagged, barely able to breathe. Chronos shoved the arm away from her throat just long enough to shout, "Let go! I'm not betraying anybody!"

She choked. The arm was back to squeezing tightly.

"Oh, really?" her sister asked in a dangerous tone. "Have you seen this?"

The arm released her, and Chronos slammed back into the chair, smacking her tailbone hard against it. Her sister's hands were shoved in front of her face, and scenes rapidly flickered across them. Scenes of Kendra, Kendra, Kendra, Kendra, Kendra.

"I don't even know what you want me to see!" Chronos sputtered.

The flickering scenes halted, and a single one took its place. Kendra flipping backwards, shouting, "I'm not a typical villain! I only fight *corrupt* magical girls!"

Rhea stopped there, as if that were supposed to illustrate some sort of point.

"And?" Chronos said.

"There is no way you're that stupid!" Rhea exploded. "She's fighting corrupt magical girls! She's trying to purify the users of the magic system, which will only make them more powerful!"

"Or she was lying," Chronos said.

"Oh, don't try that with me," Rhea said. The tone of her voice made Chronos's blood run chill. "She wasn't lying. Everything she's done is consistent with that goal. The question is whether you're complicit in it."

Chronos swallowed. She'd never seriously considered that her sister might try to kill her, but now that seemed possible — in fact, plausible.

On the other hand, she was pretty ticked off right now. She wasn't going to try to mollify her sister, who had barged in here without permission and then attacked her with both a hairbrush and a chokehold.

"I'm not complicit in anything," Chronos said sourly. "That girl, as you recall me saying before, wanted to become a villain. I gave her the costume you made and I bought her a lair. Then she wouldn't let me move out. Do you want her? You can have her."

Rhea shoved her hands back in front of Chronos's face, and more scenes flicked across her vision, almost too quickly to see. One in particular caught Chronos's attention.

"Huh," she said in irritation. "She killed one of the Koala Cuties. Guess I'll have to chew her out about that."

Rhea spun the chair around and jabbed her finger at the floor. "So you admit it! You're a traitor!"

"I don't want her to kill children," Chronos said flatly. "How does that make me a traitor?"

"How does —?" Rhea sputtered, speechless.

"How does that make me a traitor if it didn't make me one before?" Chronos clarified. "I'm not doing anything different from what I've always done."

Rhea waved her arm incredulously to indicate the plotting room and possibly the rest of the lair. "You call *this* 'not doing anything different'?"

Chronos shrugged. "Okay, fine. I saw a future where most of the world was destroyed. I acted to stop it. How does that make me a traitor?"

"*Destroyed?*" A red flush swept across Rhea's cheeks. "That would have made conditions *ripe* for our family to take over!"

"No, Rhea," Chronos said flatly. "In that future, all our family was dead."

Shock chased incredulity chased disbelief across Rhea's face. "Dead?"

"That's right," Chronos said with satisfaction. She loved when she could shock her sister. It was so difficult to do. "With magical girls ruling the world. Kendra would have been the ringleader, and she would have led an extermination against all born mages, especially villain families. Bet you'd have loved *that* society."

"Impossible," Rhea said, recovering. "We're superior. Born mages have a manifest destiny —"

Chronos jerked her hands upwards and slammed a series of visions into her sister's face.

Olympus Estates in ruins.

The Magical Girl Union.

The assassination of Emperor Kami.

The slaughter of a dozen Deathwaves.

The shattered moon across the sky.

The dead body of Rhea's minion, with a random magical girl standing over her.

"And that's only the futures that weren't totally prevented," Chronos said at last. "A lot worse would have happened if I hadn't stopped her. Believe me, villains are safer, and so is everybody else, right now."

"Why didn't you just kill her?" Rhea demanded.

Chronos stared at her incredulously. "Because I don't believe in killing children!"

"That's not a child," Rhea said scornfully. "That's an extremist."

"Fine, then I don't believe in killing *people,*" Chronos growled.

Rhea shook her hair, as if to clear her head. "That's all a bunch of nonsense, anyway. Magical girls defeating all the villain families? No way. You've got to be lying."

"How could I possibly be *lying?*" Chronos snapped. "I showed you exactly what I've seen!"

"*I* use my power to lie all the time!" Rhea said sharply. "Take things out of context, add a little editing and splicing . . ."

"Guess what, Rhea?" Chronos asked, glaring. "I'm not you."

"That's right. You're not. I'm limited to only things that have actually happened. You have *possibilities* to work with. You could easily take something near-impossible and pretend it's the most likely future."

"What reason would I have for doing that?"

"You tell me," Rhea challenged.

"No reason whatsoever!"

"Well, I *know* you're not above exaggerating!"

"I'm not exaggerating this, Rhea! That branch of futures was one of the ten most likely! The world was in serious danger!"

There was silence for a moment while they glared at one another.

"You realize I could take this to the family," Rhea said, breaking it. "Let them decide whether you're becoming a liability."

"I may not be able to see *you,* but I know *their* futures just fine," Chronos said coldly. "If I ran, there's no way they could catch me."

"Not if I worked with them."

"Then why don't you just kill me right now?" Chronos shot back.

Rhea said nothing. Her lips were tightly pursed.

Because you think I can still be useful, I bet, Chronos thought, her eyes narrowing. *You've always wanted me working beside you. You think that if you have me under your thumb, the combination of our powers would make you nigh omniscient.*

And it was probably true — that was the worst of it. That was why she would never, ever, ever work with her sister, no matter what the reason.

It never mattered how clear Chronos was that they would never work together — Rhea always held out hope that she'd be able to manipulate her eventually. She'd lusted after Chronos's power since they were kids. She'd made Chronos's childhood a waking nightmare, trying to break her to her will.

She'll never kill me, Chronos thought. *She can't do that and win.*

The silence between them stretched on, and on, and on. It felt like it would go forever.

At last, an angry shout came from outside the doorway.

"But you *have* to! She *said* you would make it for me!"

"Rhea! Explain to her that this thing is *ugly!*"

Her sister's minion stormed into the room, dragging Tiffany behind her, the little girl holding on tight to her ankle. The minion held up a crayon drawing in revolted indignation, shaking a fist.

Rhea looked furious at the interruption at first. But then a different expression spread across her face.

She hadn't looked at the child's past before. She'd been too busy focusing on Chronos and Kendra and what she might have to do to her sister. But she realized now that that had been a mistake.

In the course of just a few seconds, Rhea flashed through just enough to take in the gist of the girl's life. She could see the turning points and the broad strokes of what the girl had done and what she wanted.

Tiffany raised many fascinating possibilities.

She'd been raised by villains. She had no love for her family. She'd spent most of her life alone or avoiding the people she lived with. In many ways, her past seemed similar to Chronos's, which meant her sister no doubt thought they were similar.

But in personality, Tiffany was more like Rhea.

Rhea let a slow smile drift across her face. *Interesting . . .*

"Please please please please please please! Please please please please please please! Please please please please please please! Please please please please please please!"

Tiffany was hanging on to Minerva's waist, while the woman struggled to get her off.

It was definitely in their best interest to humor the girl.

"Give the child what she wants, Minerva," Rhea ordered.

Minerva stared at her in horror, waving the paper as if that contradicted what her boss had just said.

Rhea said nothing more.

With an exaggerated groan of despair, Minerva hid her face in one of her hands.

But she obeyed. She used her other hand to push her magic through the paper. A stream of sparkles shot through the page, sending the crayon drawing out of two dimensions and into three.

It was every bit as ugly as Minerva had claimed. It was enormous, twice as wide as Tiffany's head, and it had a line of rhinestones on it that looked simultaneously cheap and gaudy. There were three feathers on top that looked ridiculous, and two more on the bottom that looked ludicrous. It was overall a dreadful design, sheer tackiness, exactly what you would expect from a ten-year-old who designed in crayon. Rhea understood why Minerva had been so reluctant to make it exist.

But they were not in her shop. This would never have her name on it or be displayed as one of her designs. It was merely a bribe to bring the child to their side. And it was working.

"HURRAY!" Tiffany shouted, leaping up to seize the mask as it swooshed through the air, accompanied by fading sparkles. She had it in her hands before the sparkles were gone, and shoved it onto her face and posed. "I am . . . the CUTE AVENGER!"

"You're not!" Minerva said, storming out of the room in a huff. "You're just a kid with no fashion taste!"

She was absolutely right, and Rhea didn't mind that at all.

Very interesting, she thought, watching the child and smiling.

Seeing the sly look flit across Rhea's face, Chronos decided this visit was over.

"Come on," she said brusquely, shoving her sister towards the doorway.

Rhea didn't resist, which was more than enough evidence that she'd been here too long — Chronos had no idea why her sister had looked so satisfied, but she knew that she didn't like it.

They passed by Kendra in the upper hallway as they emerged at the top of the stairs.

"Hey, Rhea, thanks for all these accessories!" Kendra said, waving. "They're great!"

"You're welcome!" Rhea called, waving. "Did you like the straps?"

"I *love* the buckles."

"I thought you would! I designed them to match the belt —"

What buckles? Chronos paused in shoving her sister toward the front doorway and glanced at the former magical girl. Kendra was wearing her villain costume, which Chronos vaguely thought she might not have been wearing before. Were there buckles on there that hadn't been on there earlier?

Rhea took advantage of the pause to keep on talking. "Well, anytime you want new upgrades, feel free to come talk to me —"

"You wouldn't do that if you knew what she really does," Chronos broke in, irritated. "She corrupts magical girls. It's her favorite hobby."

The former magical girl's eyes widened.

"GET OUT," both of them chorused, pointing at the door.

"Aww, does the nice lady have to leave already?" Tiffany protested, running up the stairs and flinging her arms around Rhea's neck. "She only just came!"

"Oh, it's perfectly fine," Rhea said, patting Tiffany's head. "I'm sure I'll come to visit again. And I'll bring you a new present next time."

"Lots of presents!" Tiffany said hopefully.

"GET OUT!" Chronos shouted.

Rhea waved goodbye and ambled out the doorway. The minion huffed after her, waving a long, thin thing with an arrowhead-like tip behind her —

Wait, is that a tail? Chronos thought, startled. *When did Rhea's minion get a tail?*

"And stay out!" Kendra shouted, standing at the window and shaking her fist.

"I didn't want them here in the first place," Chronos muttered. "Turn back on the barrier," she added, looking at Tiffany.

The pigtailed girl pouted. "I don't wanna!"

"NOW!" Kendra roared.

Tiffany stuck out her tongue and summoned a wand with a pink heart on top and spiraling ribbons underneath. "FIX IT!"

There was a slight hum as the barrier returned around the building.

Chronos relaxed slightly. Rhea was gone. And now that she knew to expect her, her sister would never be able to get in here again.

"I can't believe it," Kendra was muttering. "The last winner of the Solo Magical Girl of the Year competition wore one of her designs. I never would've guessed it. I know I read an interview with Rhea Korstanos where she joked that villains always look cooler than magical girls, but . . ."

"That's not a joke," Chronos said. "That's her mission statement. She's spent the last decade pushing magical girl fashions to look blander and villain fashions to look cooler."

Kendra looked horrified.

Chronos rolled her eyes. She knew that Rhea's tactics worked, but she had no idea why. Why would anyone risk their morality for a costume change?

"Well, we don't have to get rid of their pretty stuff, do we?" Tiffany cried in alarm, holding up her large feathered mask and a red necklace with a dangly piece shaped like a teardrop.

"Yes," Chronos said.

"No!" Kendra snapped.

"You do realize that they might be magically tainted, right?" Chronos asked irritably. "We don't need Rhea listening in on us or whatever else she might have done to them."

"Cool accessories!" Kendra said.

"Boss speaking!" Chronos shot back. "Tiffany, we'll need your BREAK IT power —"

Tiffany shrieked and fled, holding her feathered mask in both hands. "No one's taking my mask away!"

"I'm *keeping* the buckles," Kendra added, pointing at her boots.

"Whatever happened to me having authority?"

"Tiffany," Kendra called down the hallway, ignoring the comment, "can you break magic without breaking objects?"

The little girl stopped and put a finger to her mouth. "I dunno. I've never tried it."

"Try it," Kendra ordered.

Obligingly, Tiffany poked her wand at Kendra's costume. "BREAK but only any magic that isn't supposed to be there on the thingys and don't break my pretty mask either because it's super pretty IT!"

Nothing happened.

"Did it work?" Kendra said.

"I dunno," Tiffany said.

"Try doing it with the cannons," Kendra said.

"NO!" Tiffany shrieked.

"You can fix them later," Kendra snorted.

"NO!" Tiffany shrieked.

"It's fine," Chronos broke in. "We'll just get rid of them. If there's a chance they might have unknown magic on them —"

"Wait!" Tiffany cried. "I can use Margie the Magic Detector!"

Chronos stared at her blankly. "Since when do you have —"

But Tiffany was already racing down the stairs towards the dungeon.

Tiffany came running back with a little gadget that looked like a TV remote control. "Margie will save the day!"

"Did you build that thing or steal it from a police station?" Kendra asked suspiciously. "That looks like standard issue, and it's illegal to own magic detectors without a license."

"Margie the Magic Detector was a present from Daddy," Tiffany said defensively.

In other words, the villain who had kidnapped her when she was four years old and raised her as a prisoner for three years before he'd been killed and replaced by her second "owner." The girl had serious Stockholm Syndrome problems.

"So it's stolen," Kendra said. "We'll have to return it."

"No!" Tiffany yelped. "Margie's my friend!"

"If it was stolen, it was replaced years ago," Chronos sighed. "Just use the thing already."

Tiffany stuck her tongue out at Kendra and pushed the button on the remote. It immediately went bananas, beeping like crazy and flashing lights in all directions.

Tiffany pushed another button, and the thing went silent.

"I guess Margie noticed that we all have magic," she said.

"Gee, ya think?" Kendra said sarcastically.

In the end, they piled all the new accessories in a corner, then added both the costumes Chronos had gotten from Rhea in the first place. Kendra stripped hers off to dump it in the corner and then stood around in her underwear, apparently with no sense of shame or modesty.

This would explain why she had a nude transformation scene, Chronos thought, shaking her head. It wasn't uncommon for magical girls, and such things generally happened in the blink of an eye, but seriously. Was it really that hard to create a transformation that covered you while your clothes were changing? Magical girls in the Middle East always did.

The magic detector found nothing unusual on anything.

"Yay!" Tiffany said happily, running over to pick up the mask. "I think I'll name you Marnie!"

"It might still be safer to get rid of them," Chronos said. "Symbolically, at least, if we accept a bribe from Rhea —"

Kendra gave her an incredulous look.

"Marnie's my new friend!" Tiffany declared.

"But if she's trying to win us over —"

"Then we won't fall for it, and we'll look really cool in the meantime," Kendra said.

"You'd understand if you ever bothered to look pretty!" Tiffany announced.

Kendra looked at Chronos. "She's not kidding."

"What does my appearance have to do with anything?!"

"If you owned an iron, you'd know the answer to that question."

Chronos had a nasty feeling that those blasted accessories were staying.

Zazz looked out the window of the helicopter, watching the lair recede into the distance. As far as she could tell, all they'd done was deliver a few presents and commit a fashion atrocity.

"What a waste of time . . ." she muttered, kicking the seat in front of her.

Rhea had a curious smile on her face. "Oh, not necessarily . . ."

Zazz shot her boss a sharp look. "What did you do? Did you do what we came for?"

Rhea laughed. "Of course. And of course you didn't notice. You were the distraction, Minerva."

Zazz tried not to pout. She hated it when it was her job to be the distraction. It happened all too often at work.

"So what did you learn?" she asked hopefully.

Rhea smiled, patting the control panel of the helicopter in front of her. "For one thing, that she has another teammate."

"Ugh . . ." Zazz groaned, putting her face in her hands. "That mask . . ."

"Indeed." Rhea smiled. "But it earned us the child's loyalty. That'll be useful."

Zazz eyed her boss. She wanted to ask what the boss was planning, but she knew she wouldn't be told. Rhea's plans were always shifting when she learned new information, anyway.

"What's our next step?" she asked cautiously.

"That all depends," Rhea said.

"On what?"

Rhea said nothing.

"On what?" Zazz repeated, feeling indignant. She deserved to know that, after making that mask!

Rhea smiled. "It all depends on whether the family will listen to me."

Chapter 4
The Rejection

X-ray vision would've been nice to have, so that Florence could have looked at the school building and found out why her teammate was late. Or mind-reading powers.

Come to think of it, mind-reading powers would have been even better, because then she could have had some clue what her ditzy teammate was thinking.

Come on, Felicity, Florence thought impatiently, twisting her focus item around her wrist. The bracelet was all summoned, and she was itching to transform. It had been a long day, track practice had been canceled, and she was dying to find out if Felicity saw anything different with her transformation scene this afternoon.

It had been nearly a week since they'd fought Queen Hemlock's minions and Felicity had mentioned that Florence's transformation scene looked different. Ever since then, Florence had been looking for a chance for them to get together and compare the details, but Felicity had been too busy. It was only today that Florence had gotten her to commit to coming.

And now Felicity was ten minutes late.

Come on, come on, come on! Florence thought anxiously, twisting the bracelet around her wrist.

She was a little afraid that their magic was becoming less interesting to Felicity. She couldn't blame her; after all, Florence had been starting to lose interest in their magical girl team before Kendra left. But now it was different. Now there was a mystery to solve. Now Florence felt lost, and her best friend wasn't here to try to tell her what to do, which had always been helpful for convincing Florence that she wanted the opposite.

Florence twisted the bracelet around her wrist nervously.

Her other teammate now had new friends. Felicity had been gradually drifting away to spend more and more time with them since Kendra had left. She'd started sitting with them every lunchtime, and even though she had invited Florence, Florence had found she had nothing in common with those chattering gigglers.

The only thing she really had in common with Felicity anymore was their magical girl team.

Come on, Felicity, Florence thought, twisting the bracelet around her wrist and fretting. *Don't dump me. You're the only friend I have left.*

She didn't make friends easily. She wasn't shy, but she found it hard to open up to people. Lute Deathwave savaging her heart had made it even more difficult.

Sure, she was friendly with the other girls on the track team, but it wasn't the same. There was nobody she felt like telling her feelings to. Nobody she felt like sharing secrets with. Nobody she could ask for help when she felt shaky.

Is Felicity really any of those things? she wondered.

Another ten minutes later, Florence decided to leave. It was clear her teammate wasn't coming. She started to walk down the sidewalk, shoulders slumped . . .

"Florence!" Felicity's voice called.

Her head shot up, and she spun around. "Felicity!" she cried in relief. "You're late!"

"I know, I know, I know, but guess what?" Felicity burst out. "Guess what! I asked Daniel out, and he said *yes!*"

Florence's heart plummeted. "Great . . ."

"Ashley and Michele and Donna convinced me, and I did it!" Felicity squealed. "And he said yes! We're going on a date!"

"Terrific," Florence muttered. "Can we —"

"First I said, 'Daniel, can we go to the movies?'" Felicity narrated breathlessly. "Then he said, 'Will you buy the tickets?' And I said, 'Uh huh!' And he said, 'Okay, there's a movie I've been wanting to see.' And I said, 'Okay, let's see it!' And he said, 'Cool. Nice to see you again, Flossie.' And I said, 'It's Felicity.' And he said, 'Oh, right, Felicity. Nice hairthings.' HE SAID 'NICE HAIRTHINGS'! EEEEEEEE! I think he's madly in love with me!"

He didn't even offer to buy the tickets? Florence thought sourly. *What a cad.*

"So now I've got to get to the theater and buy us tickets!" Felicity squealed, hopping up and down.

"*After* practice, you mean?" Florence asked sharply, holding up her focus item. She'd spun the bracelet so many times, it'd left white scratches around her wrist.

Felicity looked crushed, but she recovered. "Okay, but we've just got to finish quickly!"

Florence glanced around to make sure nobody was near them, then lifted her arms in the air. "Pink Dragon . . . *flare!*"

She whooshed into the air, spinning around as her braids grew longer and coiled into corkscrew curls. Bat wings exploded out of her shoulderblades, and fluffy pink popped all around her in her usual dress. She landed in a swirl of fire.

"'Daniel' is such a fun name to say," Felicity was saying, giggling. "Daniel, Daniel, Daniel, Daniel . . ."

Florence felt a flare of frustration. "What did you think about my transformation?"

"What about it?" Felicity asked blankly.

"Did it look any different this time?!"

"Oh." Felicity blinked. "I wasn't looking."

Florence set her jaw. "Okay, I'll detransform and retransform. Watch this time, okay?"

"Okaaaaaaay."

The fluffy pink around Florence dissolved, and her hair uncoiled and shrank back into its normal braids. Her bat wings folded down and shrank into her brown skin.

"Pink Dragon . . . *flare!*"

This time, Felicity watched with rapt attention as everything happened again. That was extremely uncomfortable when Florence reached the split second while her clothes were in the process of dissolving from one outfit to the other. Her hair was always wrapped around her like a giant cocoon during that stage, which was the reason she had it grow ten times longer while she transformed in the first place, but sheeeeesh. Transformation scenes just weren't meant to be watched that closely.

"Well?" Florence asked, landing.

"Your wings are bigger," Felicity reported. "And your dress is redder. And it doesn't look as fluffy. It all fades back to normal at the end, though. Maybe you aren't going to be Pink Dragon anymore. You could be Red Dragon."

That didn't sound too bad. "Or I could go with something fiery, like Flare Dragon," Florence suggested.

"But then your transformation words would be 'Flare Dragon, flare.'"

That did sound pretty stupid, now that she mentioned it.

"'Flare Dragon, flame'?" Florence hedged.

Felicity giggled. "You could say, 'Flare Dragon, fluster'!"

"Definitely not!" Florence cried.

Felicity giggled even harder. "Or 'Flare Dragon, flounder'!"

Florence burst out laughing. "Worst transformation words ever!" She glanced over to see Kendra's indignant expression, because Kendra always took transformation things so seriously, but then she realized that Kendra wasn't there anymore, and her heart lurched.

"Or 'Flare Dragon' . . . um . . . um . . . 'fly'!" Felicity said.

"That sounds halfway decent," Florence said soberly. The humor of the moment was gone for her.

Felicity seemed to notice, and she stopped making jokes. "Maybe I'll power up again, too," she said hopefully. "Because Daniel's my boyfriend."

You call one date a boyfriend? Florence thought skeptically. But she didn't pick a fight. "Just transform already."

Felicity held her arms wide on either side. Her focus item, the silver ring with the pink flower, bloomed out of her finger.

"Green Fairy . . . *flutter!*"

Felicity spun wildly with the speed of a top, drilling upwards so quickly that by the time her costume was transforming, you could barely catch a blur of green and brown and peach. The blur burst into a cascade of leaves, and Felicity descended in her unmoving pose of head down, knees tucked up, hands together. Her wings flapped once, and she landed gracefully on the sidewalk.

"Nothing different there," Florence noted. *You are so not getting a power-up because you asked Daniel out on a first date.*

Felicity flapped her large, sheer green wings that resembled a cross between butterfly wings and leaves. Little dots of pink flowers dotted the rest of her clothing.

"I'm going to breathe poison at you," Florence said. "I need you to dodge —"

"Felicity?" a voice asked from behind them.

Florence jerked back, startled. Had someone been standing behind her?

Felicity's face went white with shock. "D-D-D-Daniel!"

Florence spun around.

"Felicity?" he repeated, looking stunned.

"I — I am not Felicity!" she stuttered, spinning around and fluttering her wings. "I am the great magical girl . . ." She posed dramatically. "Green Fairy!"

"I just *saw* you transform!" he shouted, pointing an accusing finger at her.

"I . . . I couldn't possibly . . ." Felicity said frantically, looking around shifty-eyed. "I mean, *I am the great Green Fairy!*"

Florence suppressed a groan. *I miss Cream Angel's short-term memory eraser.* Now they had somebody else in on their secret. They'd have to hope the guy wouldn't blab.

"Oh, Daniel, I'm so sorry!" Felicity burst out, flinging herself at him and hugging him desperately. "I can't lie to you! It *is* me, Felicity!"

"You don't say!" he snapped.

She pulled back with an eager look on her face.

"But you *will* forgive me, right?" Her eyes widened with daft cluelessness, and her ponytail bounced behind her. "I mean, honesty only makes a couple stronger, and —"

"No way," he interrupted. "I'm not dating you."

Felicity's jaw dropped in shock. "*Why not?!*"

"*Duh!*" Daniel said, jabbing a finger at her outfit. "I don't want some villain to brainwash me!"

"That's an urban legend," Florence said. "Powerless bystanders don't usually get brainwashed that much. Maybe once a year for a few minutes so a villain can use their life force to power a random monster, if that. It's much more common for a magical girl to get brainwashed and attack her boyfriend —"

Daniel spun on his heel and walked away.

"Wait!" Felicity screamed. "*Daniel!!*"

Florence swallowed. She would not have seen this coming. It was better than having a boyfriend who turned out to be a villain, but not by much.

Felicity collapsed onto the ground in a sobbing heap. Her sheer green wings drooped, and the flowers on her costume wilted. Her shoulders kept on shaking, even after the sounds stopped.

Florence swallowed, not sure what to do or say.

Finally, Felicity raised her head.

"Florence . . ." she said quietly, ". . . I quit."

"What?" Florence asked dumbly.

Felicity jumped up, wrenched the ring off her finger, and flung it across the street into a nearby dumpster.

"*I QUIT!*"

It flew all that way with superhuman speed and accuracy, landing with a gigantic *CLANG!*

"Hang on," Florence said desperately. "You don't mean —"

Felicity took off after the boy who had just left her. Leaves whooshed behind her, stripping off pieces of her green costume. In two seconds, it was nothing but a mass of swirling leaves that formed back into her normal clothes again.

"*Daniel!!!*"

The Rejection

"Felicity!" Florence yelled at her. "You can't! We're —"

"Daniel! Please! I love you!" Felicity was sobbing in the distance. "Please! I'll do anything!"

Florence wrapped her hand around her bracelet. The focus item that now seemed completely meaningless.

". . . Supposed to be a team . . ." she whispered.

In the dumpster, between an apple core and an orange juice can, a tiny ring sat, glinting in the dim afternoon sun.

A whirlwind of tiny green glowing leaves surrounded it. As if by a gust of wind, the leaves blew off and twirled into nothingness. The flowers wilted and tumbled down into the garbage as blackened lumps. The ring crumbled into ash.

Green Fairy was finished.

Wings of Justice was gone.

Florence was alone.